A Weave of Words

an Armenian tale retold by
Robert D. San Souci

illustrated by Raúl Colón

Orchard Books
New York

In memory of Patricia Lomanto,
who labored tirelessly for
the cause of literacy—
"Work, and rest shall be won."
—R.D.S.S.

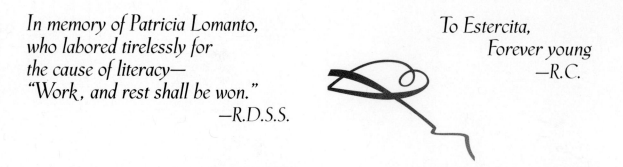

To Estercita,
Forever young
—R.C.

Primary sources for this story are the narrative "Anait" in *The Golden Fleece: Tales from the Caucasus* (Moscow: Progress Publishers, 1971) and "Anait: An Armenian Fairy-Tale" in *A Mountain of Gems: Fairy-Tales of the Peoples of the Soviet Land* (Moscow: Foreign Languages Publishing House, n.d.). In place of the evil priest and monastery of those versions, I have incorporated the inn and the red *dev* — a familiar enemy in Armenian folktales — relying on accounts of battles with these monsters in such tales as "Azaran Bulbul: An Armenian Folk Tale" in *Folk Tales from the Soviet Union: The Caucasus* (Moscow: Raduga Publishers, 1986) and "The Swineherd" in *Apples of Immortality: Folktales of Armenia* (Berkeley: University of California Press, 1968).

Background details come from such sources as *Anthology of Armenian Poetry* (New York: Columbia University Press, 1978), *Armenian Legends and Poems* (New York: Columbia University Press, originally published in 1916, reissued in 1958), *100 Armenian Tales* (Detroit: Wayne State University Press, 1982), *Once There Was and Was Not: Armenian Tales Retold* (Boston: Little Brown, 1966), *Three Apples Fell from Heaven: Armenian Tales Retold* (Boston: Little Brown, 1971), and many other works. —R.D.S.S.

Orchard Books 95 Madison Avenue New York, NY 10016

Manufactured in the United States of America
Printed by Barton Press, Inc. Bound by Horowitz/Rae
Book design by Chris Hammill Paul

10 9 8 7 6 5 4 3 2 1

The text of this book is set in 15 point Phaistos.
The illustrations are done on watercolor paper and combine watercolor washes, etching, and the use of colored pencils and litho pencils.

Library of Congress Cataloging-in-Publication Data
San Souci, Robert D.
    A weave of words / by Robert D. San Souci ; illustrated by Raúl Colón.
        p. cm.
    Summary: A reworking of Armenian folktales in which a lazy prince learns to read, write, and weave to win his love only to have these very talents later save him from a three-headed monster.
    ISBN 0-531-30053-6. — ISBN 0-531-33053-2 (lib. bdg.)
    [1. Fairy tales. 2. Folklore—Armenia.] I. Colón, Raúl, ill. II. Title.
PZ8.S248We 1997 398.2'09566'202—dc21   97-5046

Once there was a young prince named Vachagan, the only child of King Vacha and Queen Ashken. He was handsome, bright, and good-hearted; but he grew up doing only as he pleased, never even learning to read or write. The duties of the royal court bored him. He lived only to hunt, and every day he rode into the mountains, dressed in simple hunting garb.

One afternoon, Vachagan reined in his horse by a spring and watched a young woman fill her pitcher. She was the loveliest maiden he had ever seen, with her gleaming dark eyes and black silken hair.

"May I have a drink?" he asked.

She handed the jug to him, saying, "This is melted snow. Sip it slowly. You are hot and tired, and the sudden cold could harm you."

Touched by her concern and impressed by her good sense, he did as she advised. "What's your name?" he asked, handing back the pitcher.

"Anait," she replied. "I am the daughter of Aran, the weaver."

"I'd like to meet him," said Vachagan, dismounting. As they strolled, he delighted in Anait's quick wit and easy laugh.

When they reached the weaver's hut, old Aran welcomed his guest and unrolled a carpet, inviting him to sit.

"What a wonderful carpet!" Vachagan exclaimed. "The king himself has none to equal this."

Aran smiled proudly. "This was made by my daughter. She weaves like an angel. She reads and writes and discourses like a scholar. Truly, I am unworthy of such a treasure."

"But Father," Anait said, "*you* taught me to read and write and weave. These blessings are beyond price. I am content."

Vachagan said to Aran, "I can't read or write; I know no craft; but I *can* give Anait riches and power. I am Prince Vachagan, King Vacha's son, and I ask for your daughter's hand in marriage."

Anait's father bowed his head and replied, "Your highness, my daughter must decide for herself."

It was then Anait spoke. "Prince Vachagan, you honor me greatly. But how can I marry a man who doesn't know how to read or write, and who can't earn a living by his own hands?"

"But one day I will be king!" cried Vachagan.

"Times change," Anait said. "A king may become a servant. Then what good is past glory?"

"If I must prove myself to you, set me a worthy task," he begged. "Ask me to slay a dragon or catch a phoenix."

Smiling, Anait said, "When you can read and write and show me some handiwork of yours, I will be satisfied."

Seeing that she would not change her mind, Vachagan left.

But he could not forget Anait. She stayed sun-bright in his memory. And her words echoed through his mind, so that he no longer enjoyed his old life.

Finally he admitted, "Anait is right. I should master a trade." Recalling her wonderful carpet, Vachagan decided to learn to weave, as well as to read and write.

He applied himself to these tasks with the enthusiasm he once gave to hunting. But his fingers, which easily fit arrow to bowstring, proved clumsy with shuttle and yarns. As a hunter, he could easily track his quarry by reading the clues in bent grass or faint prints or scattered pebbles. Yet he often failed to draw meaning from the lines and curves and dots that made up the words and sentences in books.

But each time he almost gave up, the thought of Anait drew him back to his labors. Finally he mastered these skills so well that he actually began to enjoy creating colorful woven images or sampling the wisdom and pleasures of books. He even wrote poems. They always had the same subject: Anait.

At last, he wove a splendid carpet with roses twining around a golden tree filled with nightingales. This he sent by messenger to Anait with a letter he wrote himself asking her to become his wife.

Anait wrote back, "With all my heart, I consent."

When they married, Vachagan gave Anait a black stallion. She learned how to ride and use a sword, saying, "A ruler must be ready to lead an army if necessary." With her help, Vachagan took on much of the burden of governing.

But he always saved time for his weaving. Many evenings he sat at his loom, while Anait read aloud to him.

After several years, the old king and queen died, and Vachagan and Anait became king and queen. One day Vachagan confided to his wife, "There are reports of trouble in the east. But when I send soldiers to investigate, the people say nothing."

Anait said, "Soldiers may frighten them. Perhaps you should go yourself, dressed as a hunter, as on the day we met. If the people think you are one of them, they may talk openly."

"An excellent idea!" her husband said. "But you will have the challenge of ruling alone while I am gone."

"My shoulders are strong," she answered. "Take care, my love: the eastern mountains are desolate and dangerous."

"I promise I will return to you," he replied. And that night Vachagan set out disguised as a hunter.

After several days, Vachagan reached a village near the eastern mountains. There he met a merchant who asked, "Where are you bound?"

"Eastward," said Vachagan, "but I have heard rumors that it is risky to travel there."

"The king's men came asking questions, and anyone who spoke to them vanished," said the merchant, lowering his voice. "I warn you: stay away from the caravan that journeys east at dawn. No one who goes with it returns."

Vachagan thanked the man; but he made up his mind to seek out the caravan master. Here, the king guessed, was a clue to the mystery he hoped to solve. The next morning he paid the master — a rough-looking scoundrel — to join the caravan traveling east.

After a hard day's travel, the caravan stopped at a lonely *khan,* an inn, built into a mountainside. The innkeeper welcomed them heartily; but Vachagan saw a sly smile pass between the man and the caravan master. Vachagan laid his hand lightly on his sword hilt. He and his fellow travelers found themselves in a tunnel cut into the mountain as the innkeeper slammed and locked the iron gate behind them.

"Follow me," the man said, holding up a lamp.

They walked for a long time; finally they entered a vast, torchlit cavern.

Instantly they were surrounded. From the shadows stepped a *dev*, a creature
so horrible that even Vachagan could barely look at him. The ogre was as big as
three men, and his three heads had blazing eyes and sharp red teeth.

Vachagan saw that the cave was filled with chained men. He drew his sword;
but the *dev*'s followers quickly disarmed him.

The *dev*'s left head asked one traveler, "What is your trade?"
"I am a potter," the frightened man answered.
"Good," said the middle head. "Put him to work."

"What trade?" the right head asked another man.
"Spare me!" said the trembling fellow. "I have no craft."
"Into the pit!" bellowed the middle head.

As Vachagan watched horrified, each of his companions was sent to
captivity or death. But in his mind, a plan took shape. When his turn
came, he looked straight at the *dev*'s middle head and said, "I weave
carpets worth a hundred pieces of gold."

"Truly?" asked the greedy *dev*.

"Put me to the test and see," Vachagan challenged.

"Fail, and I will throw you into the pit myself," warned the *dev*.

So Vachagan was chained to a loom and set to work.

Without day or night, the young king had no sense of how long he
labored in the cave. He was given only *tawn,* yogurt mixed with water,
or stale bread to eat. If he fell asleep, he was shaken awake by the *dev,*
who commanded, "Hurry and finish! I will have my servant sell your
cloth in the outside world. And woe to you if it does not fetch a hundred
pieces of gold!"

In spite of little food, less sleep, and eye-straining gloom, Vachagan wove a flawless carpet, mingling yarns of vermilion and blue, green and amber and gold.

When it was finished, the brutish *dev* snatched it away. He peered at the carpet's unusual border, muttering, "I have never seen such patterns before."

"Those are magical charms; they are what make my work so valuable," Vachagan assured him. "But only wise Queen Anait will see its true worth."

Enflamed with greed, the *dev* ordered his most trusted servant to take the carpet to the queen.

Without word from Vachagan, Anait had grown anxious. One day, she was told that a stranger had come bearing a rare treasure that he would show only to her. Eager to take her mind off her fears, Anait ordered the man brought before her.

"I have come a long way to show this to you," the stranger said, unrolling a carpet before her throne.

Anait could not recall when she had seen such fine workmanship. Then her heart caught in her throat. At the center of the carpet was a golden tree filled with nightingales and circled with roses — the same pattern Vachagan had woven to win her hand. Wonderingly, she studied the carpet's curious border until she suddenly realized that the fanciful lines and swirls were really words:

> *My beloved Anait, I am the prisoner of a wicked* dev. *Whoever brings this carpet is one of my jailers. He will lead you to me.*
> *Ever your Vachagan.*

"Does the carpet please your majesty?" asked the *dev*'s servant eagerly.

"Indeed!" replied Anait. "Moments ago, I was grieving. Now that I have seen this, I am filled with hope." Then she commanded, "Guards! Arrest this man!"

Anait assembled her soldiers without delay. Astride her stallion, with raised sword she cried, "We ride to save King Vachagan!"

Guided by the *dev*'s lackey, they quickly reached the mountainside *khan*. At Anait's command, the soldiers broke down the iron doors; the *dev*'s guards rushed out to battle. The fighting was fierce, and none fought more bravely than the queen. Time and again she rallied her troops and led them forward.

Suddenly, the three-headed red *dev* himself burst through the shattered doors. Though her men retreated, Anait boldly faced the monster, brandishing her sword.

Seeing a lone woman, the ogre's heads roared with laughter. Once, twice, three times the creature whirled his club above his heads; then he hurled it at Anait's horse. But Anait caused her steed to leap at just the right moment, so that the club passed harmlessly beneath them.

Then Anait charged. One powerful stroke of her sword sent the *dev*'s left head flying all the way to Aleppo. A second stroke sent the right head as far as Chin-ma-Chin. And with a third, the middle head was spinning toward the top of Mount Ararat. At this, the *dev*'s men fled.

Dismounting, Anait rushed into the *khan*. "Vachagan!" she shouted as she ran down the tunnel.

Her heart rejoiced when she heard him reply.

In a moment she struck off his chains. Together they freed the other prisoners.

"I prayed you would come," Vachagan said.

"O Master Weaver, your skills restored my beloved to me," Anait said happily. "You can claim any reward in return."

"A kiss," said Vachagan. Then husband and wife gave each other as many kisses as a pomegranate has seeds.

So they attained their heart's desire, and may you likewise attain yours.